DEALE ELEMENTARY SCHOOL
MEDIA CENTER

The Tale of
Urso Brunov
Little Father of All Bears

For Hannah Jacques from her Granddad and Nanna.
                                    —*B.J.*

To Savannah, with love.
                                    —*A.N.*

THE TALE OF
URSO BRUNOV
LITTLE FATHER OF ALL BEARS

BRIAN JACQUES

illustrations by **Alexi Natchev**

PHILOMEL BOOKS

*F*ar, far away where earth meets sky, beyond the silent mountains, across lonely windswept plains, there are high forests. It is said a tribe of bears called the Brunov made their home there a million years ago. Who knows, maybe they still live there. They are fierce and brave, but very hard to find. That is because a Brunov Bear is only the size of your thumb!

Mightiest of them all was Urso Brunov, Little Father of All Bears. Nobody knew how old he was. Urso was wiser and stronger than any living creature—even the great white bears who live in the snows on the roof of the world.

Be still now and I will tell you a tale about Urso Brunov.

O N THE MORNING BEFORE THE FIRST DAY OF WINTER, Urso Brunov went hunting for nuts and berries. With him went some of his tiny bears, who were barely half the size of your thumb. Urso was the world's best nut and berry hunter. He gathered many baskets.

Up in the larch and pine trees lived the Bean Geese. Their leader was a fine, plump fellow called Fabalis. He waved his large brown-and-white wing to Urso.

"Did you have a good hunt, Little Father?"

Urso pointed at the baskets of brown nuts and red berries. "Fabalis, my friend, would you like some?"

The Bean Goose shook his black-and-yellow bill. "No, thank you, Urso. Your tribe will need that food to eat in the winter. Brunov Bears are hungry little beasts. I am taking my flock to the warm southlands— living is easier there. I will see you next spring, Little Father. Good fortune be with you!"

Honking loudly and flapping their wings, the Bean Geese flew from the trees. Up, up, Fabalis led them. They flew in the shape of a V (which is called a skein). Rushing winds carried them off south to the sunny lands. Urso blew a farewell to the geese on his bugle. The tiny bears waved their paws until the flock was nothing but black specks against the autumn sky.

A tiny bear tugged at Urso's fine red coat. "Our forests are icy cold in winter, Little Father. Why can't we go off south to the sunny lands, like the birds do?"

Urso grew quite stern with the tiny bear. "These forests are the home of the Brunov Bears. This is where we live. Fabalis is a good bird, but not very wise. One day he will find there is no place like home. Believe me, for I am Urso Brunov!"

In their old house of Hollowlog that night, the bears made merry. They ate nut cake and drank berry juice to celebrate autumn's end. There was much dancing and playing of instruments. They sang the Brunov Wintersong:

"Hark, the howling winds will blow,
bringing ice and sleet and snow.
All the birds have flown away,
yet the Brunov Bears must stay.
Wise old Brunov! Urso Brunov!
He will keep us safe and warm.
We, the bears of Little Father,
do not fear the Winterstorm!"

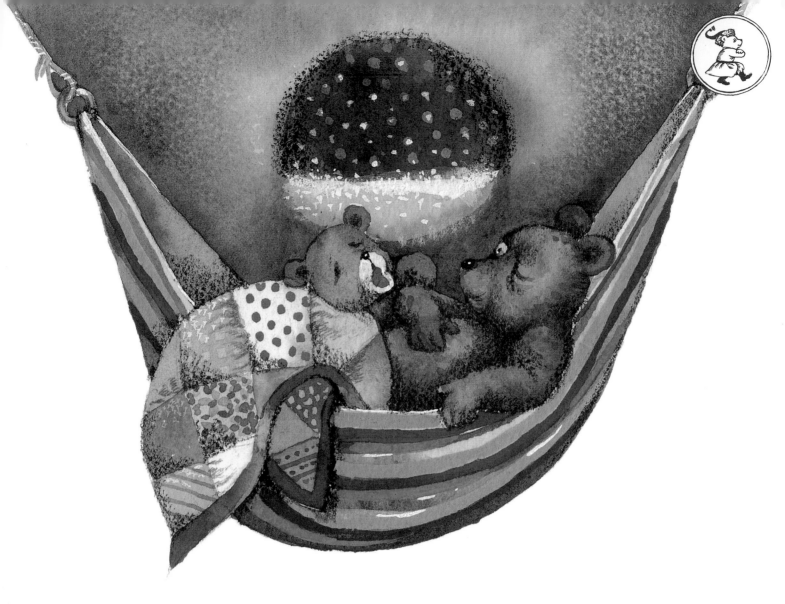

It was time for the long winter sleep. All the Brunov Bears climbed into their swinging hammocks. They slumbered long and dreamt of bright green spring.

On the fourth day, Urso Brunov was snoring like a walrus with two noses. He was wakened by a tiny bear—she was weeping and tugging at his paw.

"Little Father, four of your tiny bears have gone. While you were sleeping, they went to follow Fabalis to the sunny south!"

Urso put on his fine red coat, his great belt and his warm hat. He took his bugle and his big knife. Gently he put the tiny bear back in her hammock. "Sleep, little sister. When you wake, I will have brought those bears back. Believe me, for I am Urso Brunov!"

Outside, the snow was falling thickly, wrapping the earth in its fleecy blanket. Stars shone like ice diamonds and the moon had a blue-white halo around her. Urso Brunov blew his bugle at the moon, and called to her, "Where are my four tiny bears, O sky lady?"

The moon answered in a soft, far-off voice. "Gone, Little Father. Gone south to see my brother the sun."

Urso hung his bugle back upon his great belt. "I will find them. Believe me, for I am Urso Brunov!"

Off he trudged across the vast, snow-swept plains. He trudged for three nights and two days without stopping. Urso Brunov was the world's best trudger.

On the morning of the third day, Urso came to a wide, frozen stream. It was dangerous and slippery. He decided it must be crossed speedily. Urso found a round, flat stone. Taking a cord from the pocket of his fine red coat, he tied one end to the flat stone and the other to his great belt. Urso Brunov was the world's best stone skimmer. He skimmed the flat stone out onto the frozen stream. As the stone hit the ice, he jumped aboard. *Chuck! Chuck! Chuck! Sssssswissssshhh!*

The flat stone bounced three times and whizzed over the frozen stream, with the Little Father of All Bears sitting on it. As it reached the other side, Urso went headfirst into a snowbank. He dug himself out, untied his cord and carried on trudging.

AFTER MANY DAYS, URSO BRUNOV CAME TO A HIGH MOUNTAIN. There he met Caprix, the chief mountain goat. Bowing politely, he inquired, "I am the Little Father. Have you seen my four tiny bears?"

Caprix did a silly dance from rock to rock. "They were taken by hunting men—so were my three kids."

"Men," said Urso. "What are men?"

Caprix kept prancing about, his eyes rolling wildly. "Men are the greatest creatures on Earth. They take what they like. Now go away and don't bother me, you little oaf!"

Urso leapt onto the goat's head. He twisted its horns, bending them the wrong way around. "Carry me over your mountain or I will leave you with bent horns. Believe me, for I am Urso Brunov!"

Caprix was wild with anger, but he had to carry Urso over the mountain. Up he went, leaping from crag to crag. Over ice, snow and rocks, right to the mountaintop. Urso sat on the goat's head, holding tight to its bent horns. Down they sped, Caprix never tripping or stumbling once. When they reached the brown lands on the mountain's far side, Urso straightened the horns and jumped to the ground. He was very stern.

"Mind your manners in the future, and do not act the goat. I have let you off lightly. Believe me, for I am Urso Brunov!"

The Little Father trudged off, leaving Caprix looking very sulky, as all silly creatures who have learned their lesson do.

There was no snow on the brown lands, it was slightly warmer. Urso trudged on for a few days. Then one afternoon he came upon a group of savage wild boars eating nuts. To announce himself, Urso blew on his bugle.

Being very hungry, he called out to them, "I am the Little Father. Could you spare me some nuts, my friends?"

Snurff was the biggest boar. She looked down at Urso. "That is a nice bugle. I will give you one nut for it. One nut is all a little bear like you could eat."

The other boars laughed roughly, but Urso smiled politely. "My bugle is worth more than one nut. Let me have all the nuts I can eat and the bugle is yours."

Snurff snatched the bugle and gave a snickering snort. "What a bargain! A good bugle for just one nut—you won't eat more than that, my little friend."

Urso was the world's greatest nut eater. He picked up a nut. "I have not eaten for many days. I am hungry. Believe me, for I am Urso Brunov!"

The wild boars sat shocked as Urso munched his way through their precious nuts. He had eaten many, many nuts when Snurff gave a loud snort of dismay. "Truly you are the Little Father. Take back your bugle! Leave us some nuts, please, or we will starve!"

Urso liked creatures who said "please," so he took back his bugle. "Thank you, I would not like to see good-mannered boars starving. Now, did you see four tiny bears pass this way?"

Snurff pointed south and began weeping. "Hunting men took them that way. They captured my husband, Gnorff, too. The men have gone beyond the Deep River."

Urso pulled a spotted hanky from his fine coat and wiped her eyes. "Don't cry. Take me to the Deep River. I will go and speak with these men, they will listen to my words. Believe me, for I am Urso Brunov!"

In a great cloud of dust, the wild boars galloped across the brown lands with Urso sitting on Snurff's snout.

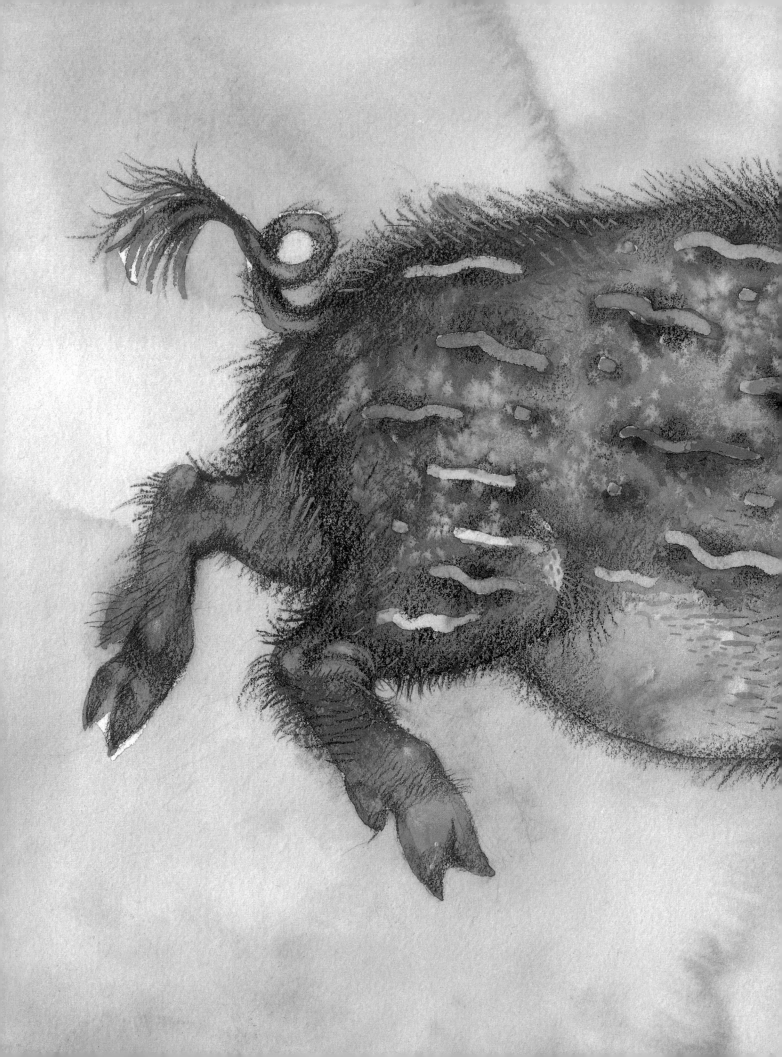

NEXT DAY THEY REACHED THE DEEP RIVER. IT WAS VERY wide and choppy. Urso jumped down onto the riverbank.

"Look at this mess. The men must have crossed here. I think men are very untidy—they must not listen to their mothers!"

Among the rubbish, Urso found a Bean Goose feather and a bamboo flute that one of the men had lost. He thrust the feather into one of the flute holes, explaining to Snurff, "This will make a useful boat to cross the river on. Wait here, my friend, and watch out for your husband's return."

The wind was just right. It blew on the goose feather sail. Urso sat aboard the flute and was carried out onto the Deep River.

Snurff and her wild boars wished him luck. "Good fortune be with you, Little Father, may the sun shine on you!"

Urso looked very noble, just like the captain of a flute ship. "Oh, he will, my friends, for I know his sister, Lady Moon. Believe me, for I am Urso Brunov!"

The wind was kind to Urso. As it gusted through the flute, he danced along, covering the holes with his paws, making a tune so he could sing. Urso Brunov was the world's best singer, even though his voice was as deep as the river and gruff as a cinder caught under a door.

"Flute tootle out tootle flute tootle doo,
if I see a fish, then I'll shout Boo!
Ho, I will cross this river deep,
my home I've left behind.
I'll take no rest, I will not sleep,
my tiny bears I'll find!
Good brother wind, blow strong and true,
the Little Father trusts in you.
Flute tootle out tootle flute tootle doo,
if I see a fish, then I'll shout Boo!"

And so Urso Brunov crossed the waters of the Deep River. Beyond this lay the hot, sandy desert.

Urso plugged up all the flute holes and filled the flute with water from the Deep River. He carried it across his shoulders into the hot, sandy desert. Many days he trudged there, sometimes complaining to the cloudless skies.

"I do not like this place. It is not cool and shady like my home in the high forests."

ONE NIGHT, WHILE TRUDGING, Urso heard an odd sound from behind a sand dune. It was a loud, sad noise. *"Unhaw! Unhaw! Uuuunhaaaaaw!"*

Drawing his big knife, he crept around the sand dune.

A camel lay in the sand, crying huge tears. Urso put away his knife and bowed politely. "I am the Little Father of All Bears. I do not like this hot, sandy desert. Do you not like it either, friend, is that why you are weeping?"

The camel twitched a tear from its nose. "I like it well enough, Little Father. My name is Gobinag. I was born here. The hunter men took my daughter from me. She is in the place of the Lightning Flash and Two Cartwheels where the Lord of All Sands lives."

Though Urso felt sorry for Gobinag, he spoke sternly to him. "Then why do you not go and take your daughter back? It is better than sitting here feeling sad. Believe me, for I am Urso Brunov!"

Gobinag shook his head sorrowfully. "What can any animal do? Men take what they wish. Besides, I do not have enough water in my hump to cross the hot, sandy desert."

Urso unplugged his flute of water and gave it to the camel. "Stop weeping, your tears are a waste of water. Drink this so you may travel. I have a feeling that my tiny bears will be at the place of the Lightning Flash and Two Cartwheels. Do you know where it is, my friend?"

Gobinag drank the water gratefully. "I know the place, but all creatures fear it. The Lord of All Sands is the mightiest of men."

Urso scrambled up onto Gobinag's back. "This Lord of All Sands has not yet met the Little Father of All Bears. Take me to him—I will get your daughter back to you. Believe me, for I am Urso Brunov!"

And so Gobinag carried Urso across the desert. It was an endless sea of burning sand, with tall ridges of steep dunes and silent, sun-scorched valleys. Urso thought it a lonely and forsaken place. However, he said nothing to the camel because it was his home. The Little Father did not wish to offend Gobinag, who was a splendid trudger. Urso thought his friend was probably the world's second-best trudger. Gobinag had broad, flat, spready paws, very useful for sand trudging.

ONE BRIGHT SWELTERING MORNING THE TWO FRIENDS SPIED a dark shimmering spot in the distance. Gobinag headed toward it. "See, that is the place of the Lightning Flash and Two Cartwheels. The Lord of All Sands imprisons creatures there so that he alone may look upon them!"

Urso grew stern and frowned a lot. "It is wrong to do that. Every creature has a right to its freedom. Believe me, for I am Urso Brunov!"

When they were close to the place, Urso jumped down from Gobinag's back. He looked at the high outer walls and the iron-barred gates. Above them was a sign, like this:

ZOO.

There was also a notice on the wall by the gates.

Private, keep out. Trespassers will be slain!

Gobinag sounded afraid. "See the sign, Little Father? A lightning flash and two cartwheels. This is the place. What does the other sign say? I cannot read."

Urso could not read either, but he was the world's best pretender. "It says that my tiny bears are inside and dares me to come and free them. It also says that you must wait out here."

Urso Brunov slipped between the gate bars and went inside. Two guards with spears were sleeping on either side of the gates. Urso trudged past them, shaking his head. "It is not even winter and they are both snoring. Men are lazy creatures, sleeping through the summer like that!"

Inside the walls was a palace, with domes, spires and minarets. Around its edges were many locked iron cages. Each one contained a miserable-looking animal. Urso checked the cages, but nowhere could he see his tiny bears.

He questioned a mournful elephant. "Ho there, little brother, where are my four tiny bears?"

The elephant pointed his trunk at the palace. "In there!"

Urso drew his long knife from his broad belt. "Then I must go and free them, for I am the Little Father of All Bears."

A great black bear called out to Urso from his cage. "Little Father, can you free us, too?"

Urso nodded. "I can free any animal. Believe me, for I am Urso Brunov!"

Urso Brunov was the world's best lock picker. He opened every lock on every cage with a secret twist of his long knifepoint. He released the black bear, elephant, tiger, lion, leopard, snakes, eagles, hawks, apes, wolves, a giraffe, a young camel, some small moun-tain goats, a wild boar and many other animals.

Urso warned them not to make a noise. "Be quiet, brothers and sisters. Stay out here, round the guards up and lock them in your cages. I am going into that palace. When you hear me give two toots on my bugle, come and join me."

A hyena laughed. "Heeheehee, I am happy again!"

The huge black bear silenced him with a stare, then bowed low in front of the Little Father. "We will be ready. We believe you, for you are Urso Brunov!"

*I*NSIDE THE PALACE IT WAS RICH AND GRAND. PARROTS and doves flew about in a beautiful garden that had a pool and a fountain. Urso had a good drink at the pool, then took off his clothes and showered in the fountain. Then he brushed the dust from his black hat and fine red coat with a small, friendly caterpillar. He could hear laughter and voices from the dining hall.

So, feeling tidy and refreshed, he trudged off to see what all the noise was about.

The Lord of All Sands wore a fez, a round hat with a tassel. He had an enormous moustache, long, thin and twisted. He was a huge man with a bloated stomach. The Lord was having dinner with his hunters, rough-looking fellows. There was much wonderful food on the table.

And also a small birdcage containing four tiny bears who were weeping pitifully!

The Lord poked at the tiny bears with a toothpick, making them cry louder. He laughed wickedly. "Do not fret, tiny ones, you are far too rare and valuable to eat. Dance for me, and tomorrow you shall share the leg of a plump Bean Goose. My hunters caught a flock of them resting by the Deep River."

Suddenly, a voice like a thunderclap roared out, "I think you are a bad and foolish man!"

The Lord glared at his chief hunter. "I will have you slain for talking to me like that!"

The chief hunter shook with fear. "Mercy, Lord, it was not I who spoke!"

Banging his fist on the table, the Lord shouted, "Which of you hunters was it? Come on, own up!"

Urso stepped out from behind a bunch of grapes, looking stern. "It was I, the Little Father of All Bears!"

The Lord of All Sands was astonished. He spread his hands on the table in front of Urso. "You impudent maggot! Little Father of All Bears, eh? You are the one those tiny bears have been crying out for!"

He picked Urso up, holding him close to his face so he could take a better look at the bold little creature. "So, you have come to insult the Lord of All Sands and take your tiny bears from me. I could squash you in my hands like an ant!"

Threats did not frighten Urso. He growled at the big man. "I am not an ant, as you soon will find out. I will take back my tiny bears and free all the other creatures who are prisoners here. Believe me, for I am Urso Brunov!"

Quick as a flash, Urso popped out of the Lord's grip. He seized the man's long moustache and swiftly bound his thumbs to it, one on either side of his nose. Urso tied special moustache knots (known only to Brunov Bears—there was no getting away from such knots). The Lord of All Sands tried tugging his thumbs free, but the pain brought tears to his eyes. He tugged and pulled until he was blubbering like a baby. Urso jumped back onto the table, landing on a nice soft loaf of bread.

The Lord stamped his feet like a spoilt child, wailing to his hunters, "Get that bear, slay him! Call out my guards!"

Urso took out his bugle and blew two loud toots.

In a stampede of hooves and paws, the animals rushed into the palace. They began chasing the Lord of All Sands and his hunters. Some of the men dived into the pond, where they met two smiling crocodiles and a hippo. Others hid in the gardens, alongside a tiger, a leopard, a wild boar and a black bear.

Some hunters climbed the palm trees, where eagles, hawks and apes were waiting for them. A few sly hunters slid under the table. A few sly snakes and wolves slid under with them. The elephant hooked his tusks through the back of the Lord's baggy trousers and held him high in the air.

"What shall I do with this one, Little Father?"

Urso blew upon his bugle, calling to all the animals, "Do not harm the men, keep them here!"

He released the tiny bears from their birdcage. "Come out, my tiny ones, help yourselves to this good food. I must go and see if my friends are safe. Eat up now, the food is free, you are free. Believe me, for I am Urso Brunov!"

Out in the kitchens, the cooks huddled in a corner, guarded by young mountain goats and a noble lion. Urso opened the poultry pens—out came a rooster and some hens, two ducks and a magnificent peacock. Then Fabalis waddled out, followed by his flock of Bean Geese. They all looked extra plump.

Fabalis felt rather fat and foolish. "My thanks to you for our freedom, Little Father. The men were fattening us up for tomorrow's dinner."

Urso chuckled at his old friend. "I hope you are not too fat to fly. It is a long journey back to the high forests. Believe me, for I am Urso Brunov!"

> Freedom, freedom, O what a lovely word,
> no more iron bars or locks,
> free as a happy bird!
> Not shut or chained in prison,
> our spirits have arisen,
> all thanks to you for liberty,
> Little Father who set us free!

That night inside the palace of the Lord of All Sands, the animals feasted and sang. Gobinag was there, reunited with his daughter. The hyenas' laughter soon caught on, and they all roared with laughter. They danced on the tables and, if they were tired, slept in the finest of beds. Joyful snores drifted up, out of the windows, into the still desert night.

Urso Brunov took a silken curtain and made a hammock for the tiny bears. They thanked him.

"Little Father, we are sorry for running away from home. We promise never again to cause you trouble."

Urso smiled. "Tiny bears have always been trouble. I know because once I was a tiny bear myself. Sleep now, dream of our high forests and home. There is nowhere like home. Believe me, for I am Urso Brunov!"

The Lord of All Sands felt very silly, locked in a cage with his baggy trouser bottom torn and his thumbs still tied to his moustache. Tears streamed from his eyes.

In the other cages, the hunters, cooks and guards glared at him and muttered angrily, "Great silly fool, it is all his fault. Hey there! No more will we call you Lord. From now on you are Old Breezy Bottom, Crybaby, Twisty Moustache. What do you think of that?"

The Lord of All Sands had only two things to say. "Boo hoo!"

Next morning Urso took all the animals outside, onto the hot desert sand. Four apes had decided to stay on at the palace. One of them (wearing the Lord's fez hat) had rearranged the sign over the gate. It now looked like this.

O, NO

The ape with the hat grinned. "We will take care of the men until they have learned their lesson, Little Father. A bit of time in cages might make them more civilized and ready to live better on this earth with others."

Urso thanked the apes for their thoughtfulness. Then he addressed the rest of the animals. "You are free to go to your homes now. Gobinag, my friend, take Gnorff the wild boar and the young mountain goats with you. Gnorff, when you reach your home, take the goats to Caprix, their father, who lives on the mountains. The rest of you, safe journey, live long and be happy. Happiness is a good thing. Believe me, for I am Urso Brunov!"

Urso loaded his tiny bears onto the backs of four Bean Geese. He climbed up onto the back of Fabalis. "Take us home, my good friend!"

With loud honking and flapping of wings, Fabalis and his flock rose into the warm air. Up, up they went, soaring high. Below them on the sands, the walled palace dwindled to a speck of coal upon a golden carpet. Over the desert they winged, passing the Deep River and crossing the brown lands. Rising even higher, the Bean Goose flock passed over the snowcapped mountains. Beyond the mountains, green patches were showing through the ice of the windswept plains.

"Spring is coming!" said the Little Father. "Believe me, for I am Urso Brunov!"

They arrived back at the high forests by night. The moon gazed down at them and smiled. "I see you have brought back your tiny bears, Little Father."

Urso put a paw to his lips. "Do not wake my tiny ones, O sky lady, they are sleeping."

He carried the tiny bears inside their home, which is called Hollowlog, and tucked them up in their hammocks. Then Urso climbed into his own hammock and slept. It had been a long journey, but he was glad that he had made it.

Dawn arrived early, fresh and bright, with small birds singing out their hearts in the trees. All the Brunov Bears leapt from their hammocks, skipping joyfully about.

"It is spring, winter has gone. Wake up, Little Father!"

The four tiny bears began telling their story to the others, of how they were captured, and how Urso rescued them. Urso lay in his hammock and opened one eye.

"What a funny story—you must have dreamt it all. You have been here with me, asleep all winter, like good Brunov Bears."

The tiny bears looked puzzled. They did not notice the twinkle in their Little Father's eye. But the tiny bear maid, who had seen them run away, did. She knew Urso did not want to upset his tribe by telling them they had been sleeping while four tiny bears were lost. She sat on the edge of Urso's hammock and whispered to him, "Truly you are the wisest Little Father in all the world!"

He tickled her beneath the chin. "I am also the strongest, cleverest, bravest, fiercest bear that ever lived. And the most modest, too. Believe me, for I am Urso Brunov!"

Patricia Lee Gauch, EDITOR

Text copyright © 2003 by The Redwall La Dita Co., Ltd.
Illustrations copyright © 2003 by Alexi Natchev
All rights reserved. This book, or parts thereof, may not be reproduced in any form without permission in writing from the publisher, PHILOMEL BOOKS, a division of Penguin Young Readers Group, 345 Hudson Street, New York, NY 10014. Philomel Books, Reg. U.S. Pat. & Tm. Off.
The scanning, uploading and distribution of this book via the Internet or via any other means without the permission of the publisher is illegal and punishable by law. Please purchase only authorized electronic editions, and do not participate in or encourage electronic piracy of copyrighted materials. Your support of the author's rights is appreciated.
Published simultaneously in Canada.   Manufactured in China by South China Printing Co. Ltd.
Designed by Semadar Megged.   Text set in 13.5-point Caslon 3.   The art was done in watercolor.
Library of Congress Cataloging-in-Publication Data
Jacques, Brian.   The tale of Urso Brunov: Little Father of All Bears / Brian Jacques ;
illustrated by Alexi Natchev.   p. cm.   Summary: Urso Brunov or Little Father, a bear the size of a thumb, saves a group of animals from a misguided baggy-trousered crybaby known as the Lord of All Sands.
[1. Bears—Fiction. 2. Animals—Fiction. 3. Zoos—Fiction. 4. Tall tales.] I. Natchev, Alexi, ill. II. Title.
PZ7.J15317 Tal 2003   [E]—dc21   2002015934
ISBN 0-399-23762-3
10 9 8 7 6 5 4 3 2 1
First Impression

DEALE ELEMENTARY SCHOOL
MEDIA CENTER